espresso
education

Phonics

Sal's Red Sock

Sue Graves

W
FRANKLIN WATTS
LONDON•SYDNEY

First published in 2011 by
Franklin Watts
338 Euston Road
London NW1 3BH

Franklin Watts Australia
Level 17/207 Kent Street
Sydney NSW 2000

Text and illustration © Franklin Watts 2011

The Espresso characters are originated and
designed by Claire Underwood and Pesky Ltd.

The Espresso characters are the property of
Espresso Education Ltd.

A CIP catalogue record for this book is
available from the British Library.

ISBN: 978 1 4451 0421 8 (hbk)
ISBN: 978 1 4451 0437 9 (pbk)

Illustrations by Artful Doodlers Ltd.
Art Director: Jonathan Hair
Series Editor: Jackie Hamley
Series Designer: Matthew Lilly

Printed in China

Franklin Watts is a division of
Hachette Children's Books,
an Hachette UK company.

www.hachette.co.uk

Level 1 50 words
Concentrating on CVC words plus and, the, to

Level 2 70 words
Concentrating on double letter sounds and new letter
sounds (ck, ff, ll, ss, j, v, w, x, y, z, zz) plus no, go, I

Level 3 100 words
Concentrating on new graphemes (qu, ch, sh, th, ng,
ai, ee, igh, oa, oo, ar, or, ur, ow, oi, ear, air, ure, er)
plus he, she, we, me, be, was, my, you, they, her, all

Level 4 150 words
Concentrating on adjacent consonants (CVCC/CCVC
words) plus said, so, have, like, some, come, were, there,
little, one, do, when, out, what

Dad has to pick up Nan.
But he has not got his sock.

It is not in the bed.

It is not in Sal's box.

Sal's red
sock is
in the box.

6

Dad pulls and pulls.
Mum pulls and pulls.
But the sock will not fit.

Sal pulls and pulls and *pulls!*
Sal gets the sock on Dad.

Dad picks up Nan.

13

Puzzle Time

Match the words that rhyme to the pictures!

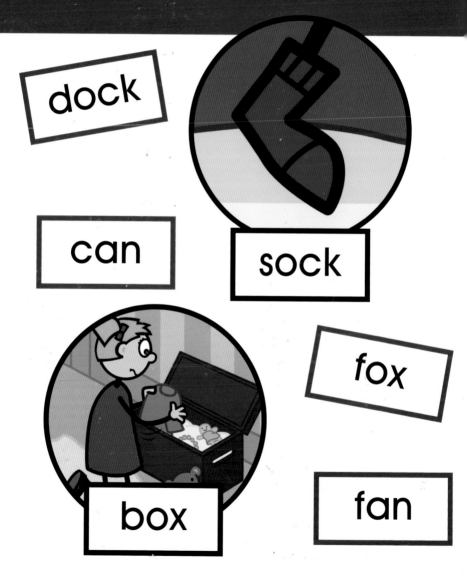

dock

can

sock

fox

box

fan

man

pull

lock

bull

rock

Nan

full

Answers

sock – dock,   **pull** – bull, full

lock, rock   **Nan** – can, fan, man

box – fox

Espresso Connections

This book may be used in conjunction with the Literacy area on Espresso to secure children's phonics learning. Here are some suggestions.

Word Machine
Encourage children to play the Word Machine Level 1. Demonstrate how the machine works, and then move on to the activities.

Ask children to find the correct first letter.
Then ask children to find the correct last letter.
Then ask children to find the correct middle letter.

Check that children are able to hear the difference between the letter sounds as different words come up.

Praise plausible attempts, such as substituting the letter "k" for "c" when attempting to find the hard c sound.

Finally, ask children to find all the letters of the word.

Spot the Word
Choose a book from the Big Book selection, for example **"Places we like to visit"** to play Spot the Word.

Give children pieces of paper with the high frequency words **and** or **the** or **to** or **I**. (The class could be split, with groups of children looking for different words.)

Ask children to note down on the paper each time they have seen or heard the word they are looking for.

At the end of the book, children should count up how many times their target word has been used.

Go back through the book together and see whether they got it right.

Praise plausible attempts, for example "they" for "the" and take the opportunity to point out why these words are different.

You could replicate the activity with this phonics story.

16